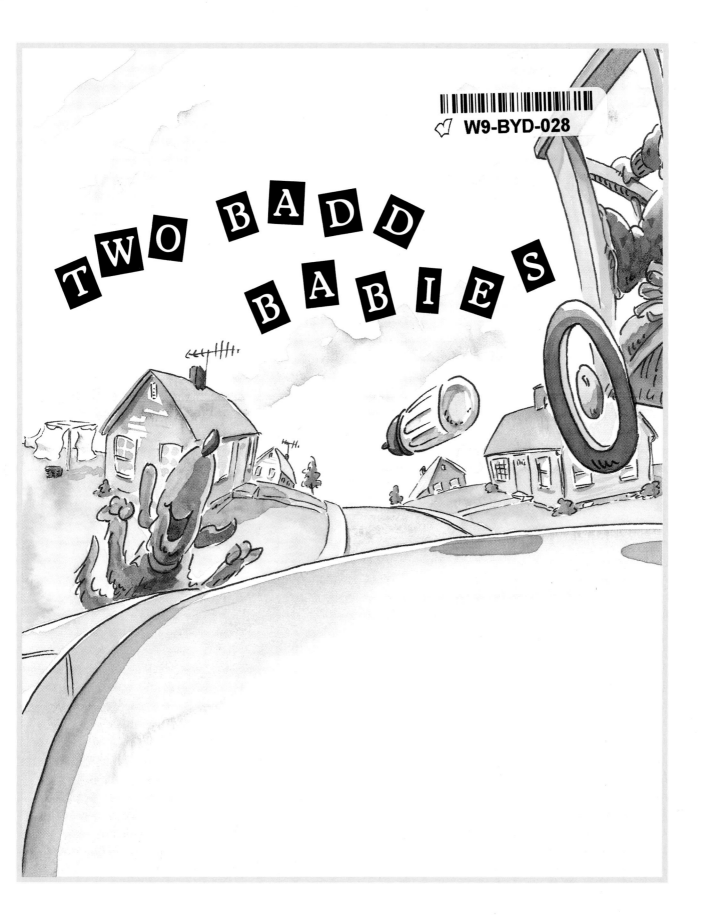

# TWO BADD BABIES

# TWO BADD BABIES

by Jeffie Ross Gordon

Illustrated by

Chris L. Demarest

*Boyds Mills Press*

*To our Moms,*
*ELLENORE and SYLVIA,*
*who know two badd babies*
*when they see them.*
J. R. G.

*For my pals,*
*Lynn and David*
C. L. D.

*Text © 1992 by Judith Ross Enderle and Stephanie Gordon Tessler*

*Illustrations © 1992 by Chris L. Demarest*

*Published by Caroline House*

*Boyds Mills Press, Inc.*

*A Highlights Company*

*815 Church Street*

*Honesdale, Pennsylvania 18431*

*Printed in China*

*Publisher Cataloging-in-Publication Data*

*Gordon, Jeffie Ross.*

  *Two Badd babies / by Jeffie Ross Gordon ; illustrated by Chris L. Demarest.*

*[32]p. : col. ill. ; cm.*

*Summary: Two babies of Mr. and Mrs. Badd bounce and rock their carriage from their bedroom to the bakery, the movies, the hamburger shack, the bookstore, and home again. Lively illustrations complement the rhythmic text.*

*ISBN 1-56397-895-4*

*1. Picture books for children. I. Demarest, Chris L., ill. II. Title.*

                   *[E]*                    *1992*

*Library of Congress Catalog Card Number 91-72869*

*First Boyds Mills Press paperback edition, 2000*

*Book designed by Joy Chu*

*10 9 8 7 6 5 4 3 2 1*

"**N**ap time," said Mrs. Badd.
And she plunked her two Badd babies into bed.

But the two Badd babies didn't want to nap.
So they rocked and bounced

And they bounced and rocked
Till their baby bed rolled across the floor

And out the door

And bumpity, bumpity, bump
Down the hill
To the center of town

Where it stopped—kerthump!
At the Tasty Pastry Bakery Shoppe.

"Why, it's the two Badd babies!"
said Mrs. Tasty Pastry.
And she gave them cookies with frosting on top
From the Tasty Pastry Bakery Shoppe
And a chocolate éclair to share.

Then the two Badd babies rocked and bounced
And they bounced and rocked
Till their baby bed rolled across the floor

And out the door

And bumpity, bumpity, bump
Down the street in the center of town

Till it stopped—kerthump!
At the super brand-new Bijou show.

"Why, it's the two Badd babies!"
said Ms. Lulu Sue Bijou.
And she gave them seats in the very first row
of the super brand-new Bijou show
And a tub of popcorn to share.

Then the two Badd babies rocked and bounced

And they bounced and rocked

Till their baby bed rolled across the floor

And out the door

And bumpity, bumpity, bump
Down the street to the edge of town

Till it stopped—kerthump!
At Greasy Jack's Hamburger Shack.

"Why, it's the two Badd babies!"
said Greasy Jack.
And he gave them each a burger with cheese

Plus a strawberry malt with two straws please
And an order of fries to share.

Then the two Badd babies rocked and bounced
And they bounced and rocked
Till their baby bed rolled across the floor
And out the door

And bumpity, bumpity, bump
Up the street to the center of town

Till it stopped—kerthump!
At the Noah Badd Read-A-Book Nook.

"Why, it's my two Badd babies,"
said Noah Badd, their dad.
And he gave them each a nap-time book
From the shelf of the Noah Badd Read-A-Book Nook.
And a peppermint sucker to share.

Then the two Badd babies rocked and bounced
And bounced and rocked
Till their baby bed rolled across the floor
And out the door

And bumpity, bumpity, bump
Up the hill from the center of town

And in the door and across the floor
Of their very own home
Where they stopped—kerthump!
And they fell asleep—kerplunk!

"What good Badd babies," said Mrs. Badd.
And took books and toys from their baby bed.
She gave each of her babies a kiss on the head
And a nice big blanket to share.